# SESAME STREET
## Let's Read Together

### with Elmo and Friends

The DALMATIAN PRESS and PIGGY TOES PRESS names and logos are trademarks of Dalmatian Publishing Group, Atlanta, Georgia 30329. No part of this book may be reproduced or copied in any form without written permission from the copyright owner. All rights reserved.

Printed in the U.S.A.
ISBN: 1-61524-234-1

10 11 12 13 B&M 35782 10 9 8 7 6 5 4 3 2 1
Sesame Street Softcover Treasury: Let's Read Together

# contents

# HELLO, ELMO!

By Constance Allen    Illustrated by Maggie Swanson

Hello! Elmo is so happy to see you!  Welcome to
Sesame Street!

This is Elmo's room. See outside? There's Oscar's
trash can. Hi, Oscar! And over there is Big Bird's
nest. Hello, Big Bird!

See this hat? It's a firefighter's hat! Maybe when Elmo grows up, Elmo will be a firefighter. Yeah.

This is Elmo's bed. This is Elmo's favorite teddy monster.

Do you want to make funny faces? Come on! Let's make funny faces!

9

Did you know that furry little red monsters are very ticklish?
Tickle Elmo's toes!

Ha! Ha! Ha! That tickles!

**This is Elmo's friend Ernie. Sometimes we play horsie. Wheeeee! Giddyap, Ernie!**

Elmo drew a picture. Do you want to see it?
Okay! Turn the page, and you can see Elmo's picture!

Here it is! See? Maybe Elmo will be a firefighter and an artist when he grows up.

Elmo will now show you a trick. Are you ready?
Watch. Are you watching? Okay, Elmo will now bend
over like this...

And everything will be upside down!
See? Now you try it.

This is Big Bird. We're friends. Sometimes we try to chase each other's shadows like this.

**Here is one of Elmo's favorite games:**

Here's Elmo's favorite number: 4. There are four letters in Elmo's name, and four wheels on Elmo's bike. Elmo has four toy cars. And Elmo's pet turtle, Walter, has four feet.

Elmo likes to meet new people. When he meets them, this is what Elmo says...

23

**Hello! Elmo is so happy to meet you!**

By Emily Thompson    Illustrated by Tom Leigh

1 One tire...

...makes a swing.

**2** Two pieces of bread…

...make a sandwich.

3 Three snowballs...

...make a snowman.

4 Four letters…

...make Elmo's name.

5 Five musicians...

...make a jazzy band.

6 Six friends make a pyramid.

7 Seven stars make the Big Dipper.

8 Eight patches...

...make Elmo's quilt.

9 Nine baseball players make a team.

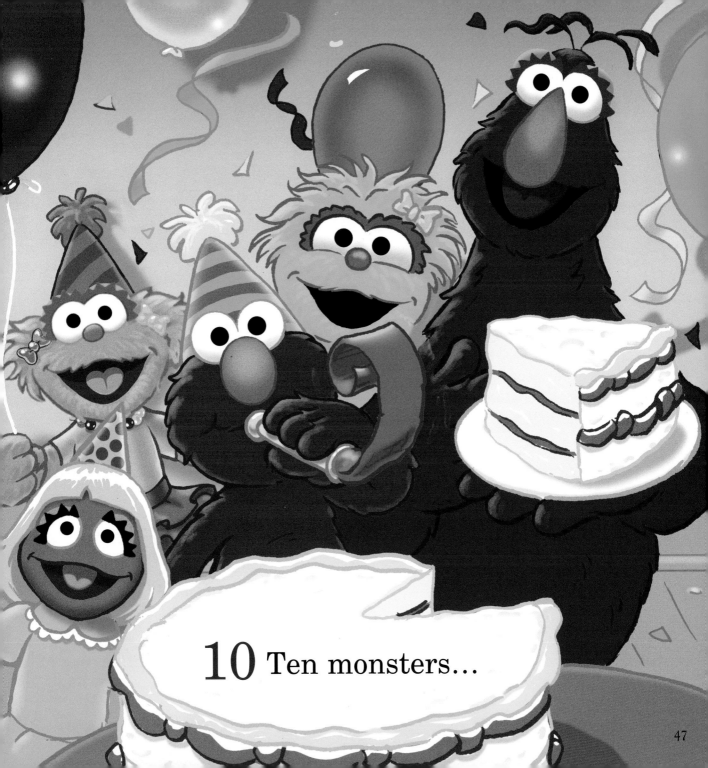

10 Ten monsters…

...make a mess!

# Elmo's ABC Book

By Sarah Albee    Illustrated by Carol Nicklaus

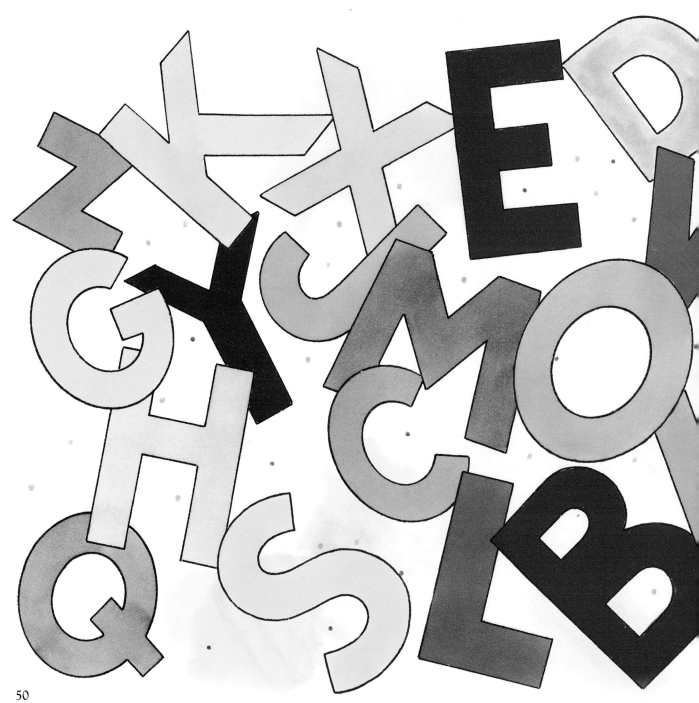

Hello! Elmo is trying to decide
what Elmo's favorite letter is.
Will you help Elmo?

Oh, thank you!

Elmo loves apples
because they are delicious and crunchy.
And apples start with the letter **A**.
So **A** must be Elmo's favorite letter.

But wait! Baby starts with the letter B.
And Elmo loves babies, too. So B must be
Elmo's favorite letter. Right, baby?

Crayon and cat begin with the letter C.
So Elmo thinks that maybe C is Elmo's
favorite letter.

Oh, but Elmo LOVES dogs! Hello, doggies!
And doggie starts with the letter D.

Uh, oh! Elmo just remembered that
Elmo's name begins with the letter E.

But Elmo's fur is very fuzzy and fluffy.
So F must be Elmo's favorite letter!

But green grapes make a great snack.
And grapes begin with the letter G!

Coming home for a hug
is one of Elmo's favorite things.
So H must be the one.
Ha ha ha! Tee hee hee!

Oh, but Elmo loves
to use Elmo's imagination!
And I is the first letter
in imagination!

Could it be J? Elmo is a very good joke teller.
Would you like to hear Elmo's joke?

*Knock, knock.*
*Who's there?*
*Boo.*
*Boo who?*
*Please don't cry.*

Elmo just realized
that kangaroo starts
with the letter K.

How do you do,
little kangaroo?

Oh, but L is the first letter in the word love.
Elmo just *loves* love!

Monster starts with M.

Elmo is a little monster and so are Elmo's friends.

So M must be Elmo's favorite letter.

Elmo can make a lot of noisy noise! Wheeee!!!

And so can an octopus.

Do you think N or O could be Elmo's favorite letter?

P is the first letter in the word poem.
And Elmo just wrote this poem called
"Q is for Quilt."
Is Q Elmo's favorite letter?

Q is for quilt.
It's cozy on my bed.
It keeps me
warm and snuggly
From my toes
up to my head.

by
Elmo

Elmo also loves riddles:

*What did the sea say to the sand?*
*Nothing. It just waved.*

R must be Elmo's favorite letter!

Can Elmo tell you a secret?

Elmo thinks that you have a very nice smile.

So maybe **S** is Elmo's favorite letter.

Turtles are terrific! And guess what?
Turtle begins with a T.

Ha ha ha! Hee hee hee!
Elmo is upside-down.

And Elmo likes to
listen to the violin!
So is Elmo's favorite
letter U? Or is it V?

Elmo wishes he could decide which is his favorite letter. What about W? Or X? Could it be Y?

Why, oh why, can't Elmo decide!

# Sleep Tight

By Constance Allen    Illustrated by David Prebenna

"Time to go home, Elmo!" calls Elmo's daddy.
"Just one more game of monster tag, please,
Daddy?" asks Elmo.
"Okay. One more game," says Elmo's daddy.

On the way home from the park, Elmo
and his daddy see lots of other people
on their way home, too.
It's almost bedtime for little monsters.

EAT AT
JOE'S

CLOSED

On Sesame Street, everyone is getting ready for bed.

Splish, splash! Little Bird shakes his feathers in his warm bath.

Sleepy monsters comb their fur
and brush their teeth.

Flossie isn't sleepy yet. Herry and Flossie do stretches.

"... Seven, eight, nine, ten," pants Herry Monster. "Are you getting sleepy, Flossie?"

Flossie shakes her head.

"Ten slow toe touches," says Herry. "One... two... three... four..."

Oscar finishes his book, *Mother Grouch Rhymes*.
  "Little Boy Grouch, come blow your kazoo.
    Take a mud bath and eat anchovy stew..."
He closes his book.
Sleep tight, sleepy grouch.

Big Bird sings his teddy bear a lullaby.
"Rock-a-bye, Radar, snug in my nest.
Time for us both to lie down and rest!
Sleep tight, little bear," says Big Bird.

At the Snuffleupagus cave, it's bedtime for Alice.
*Boing! Boing! Boing!*
She bounces on the bed.
Sleep tight, Alice.

In the Count's castle, the Count counts sheep.
"One sheep! Two sheep! Three beautiful woolly
sheep!" cries the Count.
Sleep tight, Count.

In the country, Cowboy Grover settles down to sleep under the stars.

"Sleep tight, little cows!" he calls.

In the city, Hoots the Owl plays a saxophone serenade above the city lights.
*Bee-boop-a-diddly-diddly-doo-wha-doo!*
"I'll keep things cool till morning," he croons.
"Sleep tight, everyone."

In Ernie's window box, sleepy Twiddlebugs
snuggle under their leaf blankets.
Sleep tight, little Twiddlebugs.

All is quiet on Sesame Street. Monsters and birds and grouches and Twiddlebugs sleep soundly in their beds.

Sleep tight, little Elmo.